MAKING FRIENDS WITH MY EMOTIONS

IT'S OK TO BE AFRAID

THERESA EMMINIZER

PowerKiDS press

Published in 2025 by The Rosen Publishing Group, Inc.
2544 Clinton Street, Buffalo, NY 14224

First Edition

Editor: Theresa Emminizer
Book Design: Michael Flynn

Photo Credits: Cover, p. 1 Jihan Nafiaa Zahri/Shutterstock.com; (series background) Sergei Mishchenko/Shutterstock.com; p. 5 5D Media/Shutterstock.com; p. 7 Anna Berdnik/Shutterstock.com; p. 9 milatas/Shutterstock.com; p. 11 fizkes/Shutterstock.com; p. 13 Larysa Dubinska/Shutterstock.com; pp. 15, 21 PeopleImages.com - Yuri A/Shutterstock.com; p. 17 Gregory Johnston/Shutterstock.com; p. 19 Ground Picture/Shutterstock.com.

Library of Congress Cataloging-in-Publication Data

Names: Emminizer, Theresa, author.
Title: It's ok to be afraid / Theresa Emminizer.
Description: [Buffalo] : PowerKids Press, [2025] | Series: Making friends with my emotions | Includes bibliographical references and index. |
Audience: Grades K-1
Identifiers: LCCN 2023054208 (print) | LCCN 2023054209 (ebook) | ISBN 9781499444933 (library binding) | ISBN 9781499444926 (paperback) | ISBN 9781499444940 (ebook)
Subjects: LCSH: Fear in children–Juvenile literature. | Fear–Juvenile literature.
Classification: LCC BF723.F4 E46 2025 (print) | LCC BF723.F4 (ebook) |
DDC 155.4/1246–dc23/eng/20231218
LC record available at https://lccn.loc.gov/2023054208
LC ebook record available at https://lccn.loc.gov/2023054209

Manufactured in the United States of America

CONTENTS

Feeling Afraid

When you're afraid, your knees shake. Your tummy turns. Your throat feels funny. You might want to cry. That's OK! Fear is a natural part of life. It's an emotion, or feeling, that everyone feels. You can even make friends with your fear!

Fear's Job

Emotions are our body's way of telling us something. Even though it doesn't feel good, fear can be very helpful! Fear's job is to keep you safe. If you're in an unsafe place, fear shows up to tell you "Get out, fast!"

Helpful Fear

June was walking home from school. A car pulled up and drove slowly next to her. The driver called out, asking for help. June wanted to be **polite**, but she felt afraid. Fear told June to keep walking. Fear was being June's friend!

Tell Somebody

Your feelings are important. If something or someone makes you feel afraid, don't keep it a secret. Tell somebody! Talk to a grown-up you trust. A safe adult will never tell you your fear is silly. They will listen to you and help keep you safe.

Unhelpful Fear

Sometimes we feel afraid even when we are safe. Mae wants to join the soccer team. She loves soccer but she's afraid she'll be the worst player. Mae stays home instead. This kind of fear is unhelpful. Unhelpful fear can stop you from living your life.

Get Curious

You don't have to **ignore** unhelpful fears. You don't have to let them get in your way, either! Instead, just notice them. "I notice I feel afraid when I have to talk in front of the class. It's okay to feel that way. I am brave."

OF
Oo
Ff
Aa

Coping with Fear

Teddy is afraid of getting shots. Here are some ways he **copes**:

- Teddy talks to his mom about his fear.
- He prepares himself by practicing what will happen at home before going to the doctor.
- He brings something comforting from home to hold.

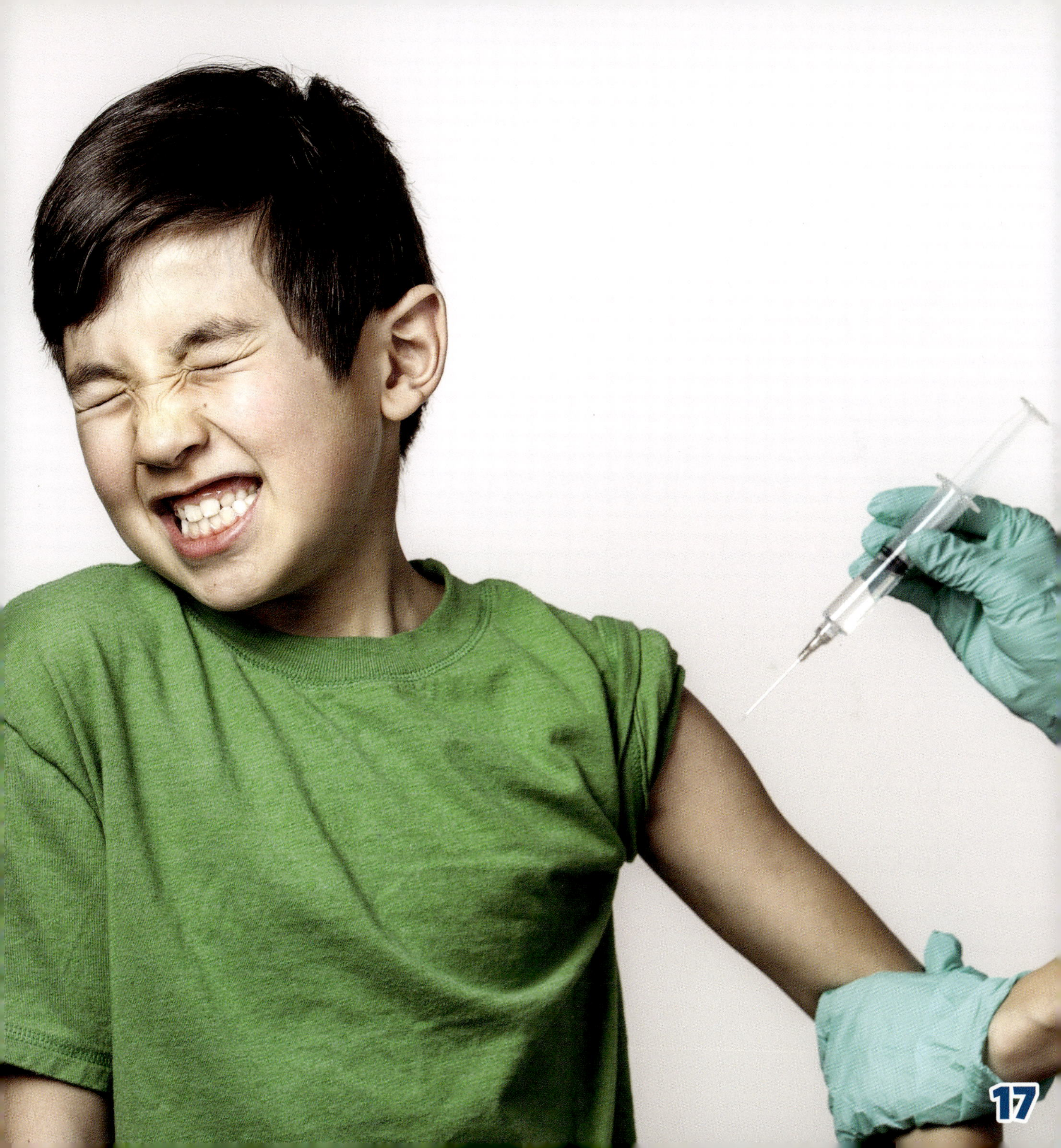

You're Not Alone

Everybody feels afraid sometimes. Talk to your loved ones about how you're feeling. Sometimes just saying it out loud can make you feel better! You could also draw or write about how you're feeling. **Expressing** your fear can make it feel less scary.

Making Friends with Fear

Remember, feelings come and go. You don't have to push feelings down or let them take over. Fear is a normal and healthy part of life. Next time you're afraid, ask yourself: "What is fear trying to tell me?"

GLOSSARY

cope: To deal with or work through your feelings.

express: To make known.

ignore: To pretend something is not happening.

polite: Acting kind or mannerly toward others.

FOR MORE INFORMATION

BOOKS

McAneney, Caitie. *I Use Meditation to Cope*. New York, NY: PowerKids Press, 2023.

McAneney, Caitie. *What Is Anxiety?* New York, NY: PowerKids Press, 2021.

WEBSITES

Kids Health
kidshealth.org/en/kids/feeling/
Learn more about your feelings and healthy ways to cope with them.

PBS Kids
pbskids.org/learn/when-something-scary-happens/
Check out fun videos and helpful activities to learn what you can do when something scary happens.

Publisher's note to educators and parents: Our editors have carefully reviewed these websites to ensure that they are suitable for students. Many websites change frequently, however, and we cannot guarantee that a site's future contents will continue to meet our high standards of quality and educational value. Be advised that students should be closely supervised whenever they access the internet.

INDEX